The Sun Is A Circle Meant For Serving

P.W. Feutz

The Sun Is A Circle Meant For Serving

Copyright © 2023 P.W. Feutz

All rights reserved.

ISBN: 9798399799568

All rights reserved. No part of this book may be reproduced, distributed, or transmitted in any form or by any means, including photocopying, recording, or other electronic or mechanical methods, without the prior written permission of the publisher.

This is a work of fiction. The story, all names, characters, and incidents portrayed in this book are fictitious or used in a fictitious manner. No identification with actual persons (living or deceased), places, buildings, and products is intended or should be inferred.

First Edition July 2023

1

An unknown number called a week after Katrin last spoke with the escapee. It had a 951 area code, so she didn't think it was someone who wanted to chew her out. She picked up and barked hello, ready to out-intimidate anyone who dared to try.

On the other end was Cory. Cory, remember? Jacosta's little brother? Four grades under you, kinda big back then, two years left of college now. Fell in with some wannabe visionaries, changed majors halfway through. Making bashful intimations of following in certain indie film-to-Marvel directors' footsteps.

He needed a capstone project, he said, but he couldn't talk about it with his friends. He wanted to stand apart, you know? He wanted to break expectations, punch above his weight, make something that no one else was making. Apparently that meant latching on to Katrin's dormant one-woman crusade against a small time, no crime cult. Nira got in touch through Jacosta and told him all about it.

Of course she did.

Resentment stewed in Katrin, and she looked for an easy way to back out, which she thought she identified when she keyed in on Cory's big mistake. He craved individual glory. He looked to her as a partner, but he really meant he wanted to go it alone, and he would end up burning the only bridges he had if he went for it. She waited for a pause to blurt out her advice, advice she'd heeded and regretted and figured she'd misinterpreted for years, for all the good it had done her. Go back to your friends, make what people want to see, learn from your mistakes, edit like everything's TikTok. Hustle, kid. Hustle, hustle, hustle.

Before she got it out, he said that his family had been involved in the Instruments of the Scion. And for far longer than Katrin's parents. They'd only left two years ago, right before the bottom fell out.

The advice died on her tongue.

"Jacosta never said anything," murmured Katrin, more to herself than Cory.

"We only just figured out what was going on," he said. "Dad's depression and losing the practice and everything. We just thought it was like going to church, you know?" He chuckled. "Thank the Scion for minority and hardship scholarships, right?"

"Does Nira know?"

He hesitated. "She only knows I'm into filmmaking. And that you could use a hand, right? I've been reading up on this Highest Seeking Faithful stuff. I'm not sure how far you've dug, but I've got in touch with an interesting group online."

"It's not run by some troll named Thomas, is it?"

"No, I don't think so. It sounds like a current member runs it, and they make some pretty wild promises."

He detailed the wild promises. Despite herself, Katrin listened, closing her laptop with its screen frozen on a blank new project in Adobe Premiere Pro.

Cory emailed his findings. The next day they FaceTimed. Not a month later, they conducted a preliminary phone interview with the group, and a month after that, they were on the road, granted an official invitation, heading for the mountains.

"Ready for some stupefaction?" Cory asked when he slid into the passenger seat of Katrin's Jetta. His oversized plaid caught on the seat fabric and stretched across his belly.

She hadn't known him all that much as a kid, but he hadn't changed. That's all Katrin could think when he showed up at Nira's door. That's all she could think as she drove up I-5, took 99 through Bakersfield, and cut east at Porterville into the Sierra Nevada. The project was underway and they were working, but he was still a little kid.

"What was the troll guy's name again?" Cory asked. He reached behind Katrin's seat and came back with a jerky stick.

"Thomas," she said. She was hunched over the wheel for a better look at the snowcaps, searing white on gray whalebacks, turning the horizon two-dimensional.

"And what was his beef with the group again?"

"Well, he went full-blown alt-right at the end, so where to begin?"

"Yeah, but what'd he say about the Bible?" The

jerky wrapper crinkled in his hands.

She sighed, tracing the opening of her recitation for the umpteenth time. "It started out sounding like the guy went looking for an alternative to Christianity and got pissed when it wasn't Christianity. He said the HSF was all about the light of God—the *light* only, and that they were obsessed with burning bushes and tongues of flame. Bushes and tongues. He thought that made them perverts."

"Nice. Wasn't there something about landing strips, too?"

"Yes, if I recall."

"That's just nuts. I don't get how guys can have hang-ups like that. The dude's got a complex," Cory said.

Katrin caught a glimpse of his canine sinking into gummy meat and grimaced. "Most dudes do," she muttered.

Cory went quiet, even though Thomas had offered plenty more for him to prove himself above. Instead, he peeled back the wrapper and chewed more softly, almost enough to make Katrin feel bad. Almost. After all, the fact of their bunking in separately assigned gender-split cabins played no small part in convincing her to spend the weekend away.

Cory never took the hint that Katrin wasn't all that interested in the HSF in the first place. Or that it was hardly a thing to begin with. Nira had forced it on her four or so months ago.

She had just moved in with Nira, having been in the valley, having not liked how it went. She bought into the hustle, or some version of it that said she could only count on herself to be professional. Assume everyone was a backstabber, delinquent, scam artist, creep, or voyeur. Use the deck life handed you. Deal out the bad cards, hoard the good ones.

The problem was, the bad ones kept popping up, like she'd lost control of her own magic trick. She taught herself lesson after lesson, did as much CYA as possible, and always ended up burned. The only lesson that really stuck was that she was too stupid and too lazy to make things work in her favor. She soldiered on, miserable and broke, wondering if she wasn't cut out for it, knowing deep down that, whether she or the hustle was at fault, the relationship was broken.

It only clicked after she signed with a real outfit and was on location for a music video, the director of which turned out to be the same guy whose indie film she'd worked on a year before. He had a new name. He'd skipped out on the film after three months. He never paid. He gave the loan sharks her cell. And here he was, signed to a legit production company, acting for all the world like he didn't fucking know her. She walked off set without a word, pushed past the producer and a gauntlet of PAs, all sneers and sunglasses, and spent the next two weeks at the apartment she shared with three sorta friends, watching her checking account drip dry until the bitter end.

Katrin expected condescension, crawling back on her hands and knees after eight years without contact. But for Nira, high school graduation was yesterday. She worked as a cosmetician and rented a bungalow with a medical emergency dispatcher who was never around, so she and Katrin stayed up late, drinking painkillers and smoking on the back porch while Katrin shared her woes.

She should've pursued online media harder or

looked into other digital alternatives. She should've ignored prevarications about toxic cultures and glass ceilings. She should've taken that archival job at MGM and moonlighted until she made an impression, or moved to Toronto or Atlanta and got lost in the wheels of industry.

"I want to make a film about something that matters to me, you know?" she said one night, feeling that her tongue had become a casket for cliché.

"What is it that matters to you?"

She stared at the back fence. "You know. The kinda stuff my parents got suckered into."

"Well, shit, Kat. Aren't the big companies doing stuff like that?"

"Not like my thing."

It got Nira's wheels spinning. Another night, so smashed that they were laughing at their coconut cream and nutmeg mustaches, Katrin went off on some dumb hypothetical, her nose down to the tabletop, grinding a cigarette into a Yankee candle cap they used as an ashtray. "What if a documentary crew was shipped off to the jungle, expecting they were gonna do some *Cannibal Holocaust* exploitation shit, and when they got there the tribe ended up having their own crew to document all the other crew's weird shit because the same thing had happened like a dozen times before?"

Nira didn't react. Instead she set down her drink and searched her phone. "You don't have to go to the jungle for that," she said. "There's something right here. And I don't mean the garden-variety bomb-the-browns and pray-to-Jesus stuff. Check this out."

She passed her phone to Katrin. It was open to a

Reddit thread purportedly started by a deprogrammed escapee of a group called the Highest Seeking Faithful.

"They call it an ante-Christian cult."

"Anti-Christian?"

"*Ante*-Christian. 'Ante', like 'before'? I thought you graduated cum laude, Kat. I thought you had a brain, girl."

"This isn't like a creepypasta or something?"

"I don't know what that means so I'm going to pretend I didn't hear it. But maybe if someone investigated it, we'd know what's going on," Nira said. Her inflection was like a playground slide begging to be rode.

Katrin read the full thread the next day. The text was littered with accusations of the usual abuses— brainwashing, isolation, exploitation—all of which were built on top of the supposed disappearance of a cofounder named Andrew two decades earlier. Commenters supplied more salacious allegations, but only a couple made decent enough cases that they, too, had brushed shoulders with the Highest Seeking Faithful. The original poster literally begged for someone from the media to contact him.

It wasn't her dream project by any means, but if it were to turn into something bigger, she might have found a way in before anyone else.

2

Katrin leaned back in her seat. She stretched her neck and lifted her sunglasses onto her head.

The trees had filled in after a lengthy stretch with an open view of the mountains. The sky up here was an untampered blue dye, the trees a dark chocolate brown with leaves like stained glass.

The Jetta kicked up a dust trail, the tawny haze of the city clinging to its bumper, but Katrin avoided looking, dwelling instead on the challenges of framing shots and blocking interviews. There was little else as satisfying as shooting some wilderness B-roll at golden hour from the perfectly scouted position.

Cory was studying his phone. He pressed and dragged his thumb and forefinger, which Katrin could tell from out of the corner of her eye meant that he was rescaling a map.

"Well?" she asked.

"About a half hour to go. I'm down to one bar."

"You send any texts yet?"

"Yeah. I mean, I am right now." Cory fiddled with the map some more until Katrin shot him a look. He started tapping, thumbs only.

"Check to see if they delivered, please."

"They have," Cory insisted. "It's a group text. I sent it to all six people at once." He took the sort of tone that got you taken off of call sheets unless your last name meant something.

"Text them individually. And why don't you call Jacosta?"

"Because then I'd have to talk to Jacosta," Cory complained. "We'll be okay, alright?"

Katrin rolled her eyes and gripped the wheel harder.

Cory dropped his phone in his lap. "Look, it's going to be just like the Instruments of the Scion, with a lot of kumbaya and passing the collection plate. I mean, think of how many of these people's Facebooks and LinkedIns we've looked at. They're all up to date, and half of them have no clue how to protect their privacy, right?" He threw out his hands. "They have business pages. With normal reviews, like a bunch of four and five stars, then a deluge of five stars with glowing comments after some jerk leaves a one-star review. They still have to play the same game as everyone else outside of their cult. They're professionals. Doctors, dentists, consultants, lawyers, middle managers. They all have places to be Monday." He picked up his phone and nestled into his seat, lost in its dim rectangular light. "We'll be fine, okay? Just keep your eyes on your purse, er, wallet."

Katrin clenched her teeth. Her first big decision in three months couldn't be to turn back and return to Nira's empty-handed. They'd eventually fight, and Katrin couldn't bear to think of what Nira might say.

She had to believe Cory was right, but she had to take his word for it, too. For as long of a shadow as the Instruments of the Scion had cast over her life, her parents had left it before she was even born.

The last half hour passed and a gravel driveway appeared in the middle of a stand of tall pines. They were beckoned by an open metal gate, above which was a wooden sign branded with the words 'Highest Seeking Faithful Retreat & Recuperation Center.'

Katrin's stomach fluttered as they passed underneath it. Its sun-damaged homeyness felt too much like a trust fall into the hands of someone who thought that hitting the ground was the better lesson.

The driveway led to a long crescent-shaped dirt parking lot full of vehicles, mostly multi-passenger vans and SUVs. On its far side was a large wooden building painted a National Parks reddish-brown.

Katrin's heart sped up when she pulled into the lot. A phalanx of women stood there, wearing sunglasses and catalog-crisp outdoor attire, all earthy tones and only the boldest pastels, a balm for the eyes under the bright sky. Their arms were crossed and hips cocked, like a cheer squad waiting out an argument between its co-captains, though there wasn't an obvious leader around.

Cory looked up and murmured, "He-llo."

Katrin pulled into the spot farthest from the building.

The women circled behind them. Cory spun around, rocking the car, causing Katrin to scold him just as a knock came at her window. She turned to see blonde bangs and goggly sunglasses, like 'on a yacht off the coast of southern France' sunglasses, propped up by a wide smile.

"Welcome!" called the woman through the window.

Katrin turned off the engine and opened the door. The woman moved with it, staying barely an inch away from getting bumped.

"Katrin, right? I'm Wendy. Sandy meant to be here, but she's tied up right now."

"Yeah, she's busy," came a voice from the group. The other women maintained their distance, and most if not all maintained a sort of haughty air. Some scowled outright.

One of them stormed off, followed by another. Wendy sputtered out a plea, then turned around, all smiles again. "Sorry about that. It's usually a longer process before anyone comes to camp. But they'll just have to get used to it!" She made a manic smile and clapped her hands on her thighs before turning towards Cory. "And you must be the gentleman we've heard about!"

Katrin left Cory to fend for himself. She hauled her gear bag and duffel out of the trunk. One of the women approached to take the gear bag.

"No, thank you," said Katrin, hiking it up onto her shoulder.

The woman shrank away.

"Sorry, force of habit," Katrin said. After another second, she handed the woman her duffel full of clothes. She had to admit she was relieved by the cool reception. It was unvarnished honesty, an automatic distancing that made her feel safer about their intentions. And if it predicted a running aloofness that kept them from capturing any damning footage, that was just fine, too.

Cory might squirm over his grades and his personal brand or whatever the hell he was so obsessed with cultivating, but Katrin could shake off some of the rustiness that had set in and relish collecting her B-roll in the sanctity of the woods. Outdoor shoots were always her favorite anyway. They forced you to run with what you had, keep to the sun's schedule.

Wendy came back around the car. "How about the dime tour, Katrin? Stretch your legs after that long drive." She pulled Cory along, her arm slung over his shoulders. He barely contained a cringe. Katrin noticed a tuft of armpit hair sticking out from Wendy's tee. That's right. No shaving for women, no beards for men.

Wendy, too, reached for her gear bag.

Katrin recoiled. "No, no, I'll keep it with me." When Wendy's eyes went wide, Katrin said, "Sorry, it's just how we filmmakers are. Very protective of our equipment."

Wendy recomposed herself. "Oh my gosh, of course." She scrunched her face and gave a slapstick salute. She wheeled Cory around and Katrin followed.

Walking the beaten ground around the compound loosened up Katrin's legs. She still wanted to pull Cory aside before they got too swept up in things, but it helped to get her blood flowing. The air was fresher up here, the shadows darker and cooler, the sunlight brighter and hotter. She pictured her parents walking these same trails years before. But that was a different place. Different group. She watched the back of Cory's head, wondering if this resurfaced any memories for him.

At the same time, she struggled not to hear Thomas's words as Wendy showed off their surroundings.

As little as she cared for him, it certainly proved that he knew what he was talking about. First was the building by the parking lot, which she identified as the main lodge, "where we hold services and take care of official business like—"

—snaring you with all the agreed-upon points of major Christian denominations, so no one can disagree. There's not one objection they couldn't weasel—

"—out there is our chapel for private reflection and meditation. That's also where we—"

—chuck in some Buddhist mindfulness and New Age positivity to make people feel worse about themselves if they're having a bad day, and you got the perfect recipe for these upper-crust lapsed Christians to remind themselves why they're lucky to be here—

"—is our recreation center. Right beside that is our pavilion if we want to take the party outside. We have exercise classes, movie nights, theater performances, potlucks—"

—kabuki prayer, which I did countless times and can't even begin to explain. They got this Japanese line-dancing shtick they do. Meditative ping-pong, regular THX-1138 *viewing nights. And believe me, it's all tied to their beliefs somehow. It's heresy to skip—*

"—out here is my favorite spot."

Wendy turned onto a trail that led away from the compound and the curious looks of bustling campers. The ground dipped up and down a couple of times. Upon reaching the top of a steep rise, Wendy moved into the brush. Katrin and Cory stopped and took in the view.

Below them was a clearing nearly as large as the parking lot with a raised circular stage at its center. Onstage was a plain wooden altar, dried out and cracked by the elements. Facing the stage was a semicircle of wooden bleachers arranged along one side of the clearing, behind which was a rocky downward slope and an unobstructed view of the valley.

The sight of bleachers reminded Katrin of attending football games against her parents' wishes. Sports, school spirit, cheering, fandom. They were all forms of indoctrination, didn't you know.

Maybe, she wondered slyly, this was where they practiced 'urination rumination.'

No seriously. You drink loads of O'Doul's and space out whereas normal guys would be counting Mississippis before puking.

It was a rare custom of the HSF's that Thomas hadn't showered with disdain. Katrin realized too late how telling that was of his real beliefs. Nevertheless, the top of the stands, with that view? She had to admit it would make for a good place to unzip and let fly.

"Katrin?" Cory asked.

She blinked and looked over. "I'm sorry, what?"

Wendy laughed. "No, I get it. It's really something, isn't it? I was just saying this place always leads me back to the light, no matter what kind of day it's been." She took an appreciative breath, like the clearing was filling her with narcotic goodness, then stepped onto the path and led them back to the compound.

The cabins were all that was left to see. Six in total, with running water and electricity, sat across the compound from the main lodge, between which was a massive fire pit alongside a curved, blackened beam that stuck up from the ground and toward the pit like the angel of death's finger.

A shiver crept up Katrin's back. They'd reached the point at which she and Cory, as un-reassuring as he was, had to be separated. Foot traffic was heavy around the cabins, though, and campers were preoccupied with moving in for the weekend. They were as disinterested in Cory's and her presence as the average commuter. Some may not have even known what they were here for. Apparently the only ones with any real objections to their presence had already met them in the parking lot before they stormed off. The pair shared a look before a teenage boy reached for the backpack slung over one of Cory's shoulders and Katrin followed Wendy inside.

3

"This is good timing," Wendy whispered. "You can make your own bed and let everyone see you're pulling your own weight."

She squeezed Katrin's arm in farewell, leaving her beside an empty bottom bunk bed, but froze mid-step and gripped Katrin's shoulder. "Oh! There's Sandy right there. Let me get her."

The cabin was a flurry of activity. Women and girls chattered and pivoted around one another. Backpacks rustled. Floorboards creaked. Sheets fluttered. Plumes of dust motes glittered in sunbeams and the air smelt even fresher for the windows having just been opened. Eyes flitted Katrin's way, some curious, some judgmental.

The energy inside had the determined practicality of a zero-budget movie set, letting Katrin disappear in plain sight. The location manager in her took over, and she soaked in the cabin's furnishings: open rafters, cage lamps, a nine foot wardrobe, a clearly marked medicine cabinet. She reflexively scanned the floors, looking for gaffer tape that snaked over electrical cords or blocked out actors' marks, when she noticed that the bed frames were bolted to the floor. She followed the length of a bed and saw that its back leg was chained to the wall with a bike lock.

Wendy flourished the arrival of another woman. "Katrin, allow me to introduce you to Sandy DiMarco."

Katrin stiffened. She hadn't expected the initial meet-and-greet with the co-head of the Highest Seeking Faithful to be so sudden, or so casual.

But here she was, Sandy DiMarco, marching straight toward her, hand outstretched. She clenched Katrin's hand and said, "How do you do?" Then she turned to admire her followers' activity, drawing in Katrin to do the same, before pivoting back to show her a perfect, portrait-ready smile, with pinchable dimples and straight white teeth.

Katrin excelled at the cold stare when dealing with people on set, but Sandy wasn't like any person she'd worked with before. Her reputation aside, she was the focal point of this whole project, the subject of Katrin's story. Along with Ralston DiMarco, that was. If those were their real names. If they were even legally married.

She stammered a reply, fixated on Sandy's appearance, her prematurely gray but full hair, her stylishly crushed woven cowboy hat, her athletic build.

Myriad emotions fought for prominence, not the least of which was rage, on her own behalf, on her parents' behalf, at Sandy and Ralston and the Highest Seeking Faithful, at the Instruments of the Scion, at the man her parents referred to, if at all, in their obsessive hatred as *him*. But the rage wouldn't have been coherent to the person standing before her. Another emotion, one that blended in better with the cheery and determined vacuousness of the cabin, stepped forward.

Her face softened. She let her objectivity slip to see what happened when she made herself open to suggestion. The DiMarcos' power lay in their charm, as it did for all of these cult leaders. As it did for *him*. She wanted to be charmed for a moment, one little experiment to scribble in her notepad.

She wouldn't have to tell anyone if she didn't want to. And if it touched her in a way that she couldn't easily scrub off, she'd tell herself it was for the sake of her experiment, an admission of the filmmakers' own faltering in the face of masterful con artistry. Her impulse out-dueled her reserve, and with the breakout of a cold sweat, she leaned forward for a hug, a tangible connection to the source material.

Only, the gesture was so subtle, so private, that Sandy didn't notice, which was for the best, since she didn't begin speaking about anything particularly piercing or enlightening. She dove into a list of the weekend's special events: a badminton tournament, bonfire, and movie screening tonight, breakout sessions and group hikes tomorrow, etcetera, when the woman who'd taken Katrin's duffel appeared.

"I'll just put this under your bed," she interrupted.

The woman crouched beside her. The bag was too tall to fit, so she got down to her knees, smashed the bag down, and pushed it in a zigzag fashion until it was under the bed, nudging Katrin as she went.

Sandy slowed down, having dove into the mundanities of meal preparation. She cut herself short, wrung her hands, and said, "You have plans for us, too, yes? What do you have in mind?"

Put on the spot, Katrin stumbled through her itinerary. "Well, really, besides the solo interviews with you and Mr. DiMarco, we'd like to record group activities. Like all the ones you just mentioned, but especially the ones that incorporate your spiritual beliefs, and... or... practices. If you could let Cory and I know—"

Sandy gasped and clasped her hands. "That's right. I forgot about the young man," she said. Her brow furrowed, and she looked around the room. "I should have Ralston stop in to see that the boy isn't being hassled." She craned her neck and looked out the window.

"Hassled, huh?" Katrin said. Her mouth turned up into a grin.

Sandy twitched like she'd suffered a particularly big static shock, then placed her hand on Katrin's shoulder. "Oh! Don't you worry about a thing. It's just that you know how boys can be. They come on strong, but it gets it out of their system faster. Still, Wendy!" She took her hand off Katrin's shoulder and ushered over Wendy. "Wen, can you look in on Katrin's friend in the men's dorm? See that Ralston's seen to him? Thanks, hon."

Wendy marched off, and a teenager slipped between Katrin and Sandy to drop folded sheets onto the bed.

The flurry of the cabin died down. Bed-making concluded. Baggage was stowed. The number of women in the cabin dwindled until there was nothing left but a cluster of younger women knotting the laces on their running shoes and stretching their shoulders. They filed out the doors, tittering and laughing, looking like they were ready for a cross country race.

Sandy surveyed the cabin and nodded, and made a satisfied sigh. With a point of her finger at the bed, she said, "I'm sorry, I kept you with all my jabbering. Rule number one. Putting on your own sheets. Maybe Wendy told you, but the first step in seeking that which is highest is a crisply made bed."

There was another prevision of something warm and overwhelming between them, and Katrin expected another hand on the shoulder, half-expected a full-on embrace. Instead, Sandy backed up a step, her smile faltering into introspection, before she turned to leave without another word.

Finally alone, Katrin let her shoulders slump. She'd intended to ask for a place in the main lodge for Cory and her to use. She wrinkled her brow, shook her head and rubbed her neck, and surveyed the room for electrical outlets.

She dropped her gear bag on the unmade bed, sat, and peeled back the bag's flimsy crocodile-like mouth. Out of the flap's main pocket peeked a yellow legal pad which she removed and gazed at with disinterest.

It was the only time she had to herself since this morning, and though that wasn't so long a time for someone who'd spent countless hours on non-union jobs, she eased into the bastion of solitude and let the day's stress weep away from her tight muscles.

A new source of unease presented itself, one whose traces went much further back than the recent rigors and disappointments of the creative life, farther back than college, or high school, or anything within her recall. She'd been left behind. The campers were gone, having moved on to something they wanted to do and which she knew nothing about.

That's the documentarian's role, she told herself.

Outside observer. Objective. The ghillie-suited Discovery Channel photographer with a telephoto lens, hunkered down on the slope across the valley from the snow leopard's den.

The rationale did little to stem her melancholy. The campers' synchronicity made her sick for work. Shoots could be like that, well oiled, spiffed up, if you had a good crew, good management. But more often than not, even among the best people, she found elements of chaos to exploit, so that no matter how much downtime there was, no matter how disjointed was the scene prep, she found something or someone to commandeer, so that she could enact her vision on some small part of the production. She made it her mission, as a way to make sure she was never superfluous. The more dysfunctional the set, the bossier she could be. That was how she stayed involved.

The only chaos here was an unmade bed. After a quick scan of her bag's contents, she zipped it back up and stowed it under the bunk.

She decided to get involved. It started by slipping the fitted sheet over all four corners of the mattress and tucking in her sheet and blanket.

4

"Where the heck have you been?"

Cory stood alone outside the women's cabin. He was doing nothing, and he looked like he had nothing to do. His only inclination was to gravitate toward Katrin and await orders. It gave her a stomach cramp.

"You could've come got me."

"I didn't know if you were changing or showering or… what. Then I thought maybe they took you away or something. Like, disappeared you."

"Yeah, okay. If I'm getting sacrificed by a cult, it's going to be a show, alright? I'd insist on it if it wasn't."

"You don't know that. These people could be up to anything. Your Thomas guy said that people came here and never left. Andrew, wasn't it? Isn't that one of the main reasons we're here? We gotta be careful."

"Not *my guy*, first of all. And I got the distinct impression that Thomas spent maybe a month with these people, tops, then shat his pants and ran from the smell. Secondly, whatever happened to 'all these people got places to be Monday; they're all businesspeople'? And you were in the Instruments, weren't you? How many people did you disappear?"

Cory opened his mouth, but answered with an eye roll. If he could bring up the Scion so damn much, so could she. It never ceased to amaze her that he didn't seem to understand that she didn't have firsthand knowledge of the Instruments' nonsense. It all came from her parents. A part of her was pleased to have annoyed him, though. She'd taken her sweet time inside. How was she supposed to know he'd lay his muzzle at her feet like a dog?

The compound was devoid of campers. Warning shadows of approaching evening reached out over the dusty ground from buildings and trees. That strange curved beam by the fire pit stuck up from the ground like a shadow made tangible, and for the first time Katrin noticed its blackened coating came from ash.

The sounds of some sort of athletic contest came from over the rise to the west. Cheers and moans. A whiff of charcoal smoke reached her nose and reminded her that she was hungry.

"Anyway," she changed the subject and walked on, "is your phone charged?"

"Charging now."

"Wall socket or charger? You should have it on you at all times."

"Socket. I'm not lugging around a phone and a battery pack. That's ridiculous."

"We'll get it in a second. Any charge is better than none. So what's the rest of the plan?"

"Like, theirs or ours? I thought you had the

checklist."

"Yeah, I do, but remember, if you want to learn, you gotta have the answer even though you think I do. Right?"

"Yesss. Okay. Can I have it then?"

"We'll go through it together." She spoke authoritatively. It was nice, having a little PA to push around. "You get hassled?"

"Huh?"

"Hassled. Anyone hassle you. What's the men's cabin like, anyway?"

Cory scrunched up his brow and shrank into himself, and Katrin felt a pang of guilt, knowing perfectly well what she'd made him self-conscious about. Everyone here was fit and chipper. And they were all friends.

"Just normal. Everyone was busy and basically ignored me. I met Ralston for a second, but I didn't get a chance to talk to him. Hardly got a read on him, either. He was just sorta there."

No different than her experience. She left it at that, waited for him to get his phone, then led the search for dinner.

On the way, she quizzed him on their gear. His own kit he had well rehearsed. DSLR with 35mm lens, a rented 300mm telephoto lens, clip-on phone lens if it came down to it, sound recorder, light meter, two microphones, heavy tripod, collapsible tripod, the handheld gimbal stabilizer he bought used and that she didn't quite trust to work, an eight pack of no-name 128gb memory cards, six no-name camera batteries and two chargers, fresh packs of no-name AA and D batteries, three additional battery chargers, clapperboard, chalk, dry-erase board with markers, reflector screen, portable lights, flashlight, multitool, first aid kit, glasses repair kit, poncho, tarp, duct tape, electrical tape, painter's tape, masking tape.

"And before you forget?" she raised her eyebrow, leaned into him.

"Yes, we also have a metric shit ton of bottled water in the trunk of the car, because hydration is key to a safe and successful shoot. I measured it out myself, triple-checked it, loaded it myself, if you remember, then checked it again, and that's the number I arrived at. One single metric shit ton."

"Don't forget the sunscreen."

"Easy. SPF 45. Forty-five gallons of it."

He struggled through her kit, though it was far shorter than his. She knew he'd want to have all the fun, so she only took her Sony with the 35mm lens, camera cage, and shoulder mount. If this was going to be *California Cannibal Holocaust*, she figured she should strip things down, go barebones. Cory recalled her camera gear easily enough, but she pestered him on the specifics. How many batteries, memory cards, extra pens and pencils. What paperwork did she have. Shot list and schedule, consent forms, interview questions, and inventory. It shouldn't be hard to remember. They were out here to capture a story, and they'd done their research.

"You didn't shoot the front gate, did you?"

Cory pulled a confused face. "Did you want me to shoot the front gate?" He hesitated. The driveway was a long way back, and they were losing light.

At that, she had to admit she missed a mark, too. Cory was usually on top of coverage. He'd constantly been floating his phone around Nira's kitchen, zooming in on

Katrin's face as she stared at her laptop, collecting little tidbits of their planning. He filmed literally the entire time she packed her clothes, until she got to a particular drawer and shot him a vicious look. For parts of the drive up here, he used a grip to display his phone on the dash while they ran through a semi-scripted dialogue. Katrin kept it to herself that none of it would be used, but now was the time to get footage. They might feel like they were guests, but they had to shake that off. They were there to shoot.

Any other project, Katrin would've opted for a motel, but Cory insisted on an embed. If things went well, they'd be back. That was the X-factor. That was what would make them stand out. He thought it was so clever, using these people's delusions of their own sanctity against them. According to Cory, the DiMarcos would happily spill the worst of their offenses because they didn't realize they were in the wrong. Katrin tried to remind him of a cult's system dynamics, the in-group and the out-group, frenzied activity, unquestioning obedience to the leader, until she decided it wasn't worth arguing. Hell, the kid had gone through it himself. Either he was still in denial or he was too dumb to see it. She ended her case by insisting they would be considered a threat, if only a small one. They were invited to be there, after all. She left it at that, before she told him more than she wanted to.

She was about to tell him to shoot the gate in the morning when she noticed someone down one of the footpaths that Wendy had led them down earlier. It was a teenage boy, and he had a camera that he swiftly dropped and pretended to inspect when she looked at him.

Fair play, as far as she was concerned. She kept it to herself, and followed her nose toward the grilling smells.

Cory would only be unnerved, so when he asked if he really had to get that shot tonight, she told him he'd better hurry up.

5

The generous view was to think of the people here as campers instead of cultists, and that's what ran through Katrin's head when she found them in a field down one of the side paths, lured by the grill smoke, and braced herself for the first real test of their bounds of normality. It wasn't only generous to them, either. Katrin had to think of them as her own kind of people, just normal everyday people, to feel comfortable entering their midst.

There was enough space on the far side of the field for four badminton nets set up in a quad, with doubles matches being played at each one. There were supposed to be about four hundred people here this weekend, and it looked like they were all here. Besides their cheers and boos, the air was rife with the sounds of shuttlecocks whistling and rackets whirring. On the side of the field that faced the falling sun, campers sat on wooden bleachers three levels high, watching through sunglasses or from under ball caps or tented fingers. No one seemed to consider sitting on the other side, where a matching, and perfectly unbroken-looking, bleacher set resided, to save themselves the eyestrain.

Closest to the path, where Katrin entered the field, was a collection of octagonal wooden picnic tables as warped, distressed, and sun-bleached as driftwood on a beach. Off to the side, a group of men tended a half dozen smoking charcoal grills. The remnants of the grills' red and black enamel paint clung on for dear life against a cancerous rust. The men nudged around brats and flipped burger patties, looked back at the badminton, and, in a touch that brought her a spark of joy, sipped from cans of O'Doul's.

From among the cadre of burger chefs, someone called out to her.

"Uh oh! Is that who I think it is?"

For a brief second she feared it might actually be someone who recognized her from the real world. But then a man detached himself from the others and came up to her.

She knew Ralston DiMarco right away, despite the sunglasses and Stetson pulled down low over his round face. She'd pored over anything she could find on the DiMarcos online. In person, for the first time, the impression he made wasn't quite as sensational as Sandy's. He was taller than her by a few inches, sure, but he packed on the dense burliness of a poor diet that outstripped whatever exercise he put in. He might not be so much to blame for that, since the stiffness with which he moved suggested injuries sustained in a former, more adventurous life. It made Katrin sad, picturing a devoted couple's longevity stymied by the decrepitation of one of their bodies. Limiting her, shaming him. His handshake was respectfully firm, his hands rough enough to lay claim to a routine of physical labor.

He apologized just the right amount for mispronouncing her name, then invited her to join the cooks, telling her she had to meet some of their board members before he got Sandy to play the hostess.

"Can I get you anything?" he asked. "Water, lemonade?"

Hell, Sandy could wait. So could the rest of the group, until it was absolutely necessary. He was already acting the consummate host, and he had all the food. "I'll have what you're having."

"Oh oh!"

He grabbed an O'Doul's from a cooler filled to the brim with icy water. The can wept little lampreys of icicles that made Katrin's fingers go numb.

I'm going to piss over a cliff tonight.

Sandy eventually joined them and brought conversation that flowed mostly in Katrin's direction, forcing her to discharge bland, resumé-like answers to the usual queries into her work and ambitions.

Badminton ended in short order and a board member sounded a dinner bell. Burgers and brats on toasted sesame seed buns were the top items on a smorgasbord of Fourth of July-type fare, featuring an array of grilled toppings ranging from portobello mushrooms to grilled pineapple, sauces, dressings, fruit salad, watermelon, basically the whole chips aisle, and six varieties of pasta salad, the cajun and Thai varieties of which went fast. Katrin took what looked most agreeable to her stomach and nibbled until her plate was empty.

Cory appeared after about half an hour, making it

just in time to eat, carrying his camera in a shoulder bag and nursing a wounded look. Katrin's saving him a seat appeared to soothe him. They were planted at the board members' table, where she fielded more inane questions. Harder ones, which probed ever so slightly into her morals and convictions, were limited to the subjects of cinema, the younger generation's work ethic, and all such things that she had no real answers for and to which they couldn't pin her down to any particularly strong or divisive opinion.

One board member kept interjecting about his own son's obsession with movies, to the point that Katrin worried she might have another Cory to deal with. That did help to explain the teen she'd seen creeping around with a camera, freeing her from one tiny source of discomfort.

Sunglasses on, squinting hard past the low sun, she scoured fruitlessly the table's expressions for any hint of objection or distaste. It was like a dinner scene in a period drama, so perhaps they were making fun of her in their own supercilious way. If that was the case, she was so far removed that she couldn't be bothered to search for clues she'd never catch on to. Cory was her biggest concern, but once he started eating, his sourness went away and he was polite and shy and perfectly inoffensive. That was the beauty of catering in the filmmaking world. Have food, will comply.

Root beer floats served as dessert, and after that, the women from the neighboring table got up and cleared plates. The board members—all male, Katrin noted, which seemed to contradict Thomas's biggest gripe —all leaned back, patted their bellies in unison, and traded looks.

Time? Time, they said, back and forth, and rose heavily from their seats.

"You'll want to film this part," Ralston said to them.

The campers enacted an all-hands cleanup operation with the same ant-like coordination with which they'd settled into their cabins. Badminton nets were taken down, leftovers packaged and removed, refuse collected and dumped into fifty-five-gallon bins.

When Cory started filming, one of the men stopped him. Katrin's stomach dropped, but more at the sight of Cory's nervous overreaction than the man's gentle instruction. "Not this," he said, and pointed at the other board members, who made their way back to the compound.

From a storage shed alongside the first men's cabin, the board members retrieved a bundle of eight-foot iron poles, atop of which they affixed torch heads.

"Time to light the landing strip," Ralston said to no one in particular. "We could call it something like 'the lighting of the way,' but that sounds old fashioned, doesn't it? Stolen. Pretentious. We may as well just call the thing what it is, which sometimes just means what it feels like what we're doing."

Understanding he was now talking to her, Katrin perked up. "Sort of like an emotional onomatopoeia?" she asked, half-jokingly.

Ralston smirked. "Or an intellectual one, if the distinction matters. That's what all metaphors are. It's not to understand reality through your own special lens, but a way to transform everyone else's reality into the one you already know. We use metaphors like germs, for infecting. Or like pheromones, for marking."

Sensing that she'd be out of shot, she checked to make sure Cory was filming, which he was. This might be the start of some interesting sound bites, the sorts of aphorisms and proverbs that twisted people's brains into knots. A scoffing at pretentiousness, followed by a perfect embodiment of it. That was exactly the sort of discombobulated rhetorical trap she secretly wished for from tomorrow's sit-down interview with the DiMarcos, if only for the challenge of knitting them into coherence during the edit.

The men began marching across the compound, past the fire pit, but instead of stopping right there or going back down to the field, they went down the amphitheater path. Physically, they all resembled Ralston, collages of ruined joints and vertebrae and missing cartilage, guys that staved off aging by playing like kids, and who ended up fighting a losing battle against their own self-inflicted damage. She envied their energy, as much as she pitied the sort of person who doesn't know their limits. It told her a bit about the kind of people who came to the mountains to worship their own little god, in their minds the ante-god, god of all gods, the one all those normal people didn't know about. More ashamedly, it made her conscious of her waistband digging into her stomach. Before she was spending her days in Nira's living room, she was a lot like them.

"What's the landing strip for?" she asked, marching single file behind Ralston. Cory was behind her, camera held way out to his left to catch a glimpse of the exchange.

"The sun," said Ralston. "We want to make sure it comes back, right?"

"You don't trust it to?"

After thirty seconds or so, enough that Katrin thought she was being ignored, Ralston said, "No, we trust it to return every day. We only like to show it the way. That's what really brings us together. It's the only thing we really have any power over."

They descended into the amphitheater. Ralston moved stiffly, and favored his right leg. One man plugged his torch into a bracket attached to the stage edge. The rest made for a trail on the opposite side of the clearing.

I'm sure the DNR will love this.

This was obviously a ritual, but she felt irresponsible, complicit, not to say something. The hillsides all along the drive up here were pocked with swaths of scorched tree trunks from recent wildfires.

"Is there a service or something here tonight?" She looked around the space. The sun was close to the horizon, its marigold yellow rays interspersed with elongating shadows. The timing made sense, she guessed. They had to light the way before the sun couldn't see them anymore, right?

Sandy's voice came from behind them. "Not tonight." Graceful as ever, she caught up to them. "Katrin, why don't you come with me and see about filming the bonfire? I think the young man can take it from here, yes?"

Katrin told him to go, which to her surprise caused a knot in her stomach. He stared at her with doubt creasing his eyebrows, but she wanted to show some trust in their hosts and turned to follow Sandy. Upon reaching the section of trail where they would lose sight of the clearing, the knot hadn't undone itself. She looked back, but he was already gone.

6

Sitting around the fire pit, some younger children ripped up scrap paper for kindling while older volunteers built a cabin-teepee structure from bundles of brush and wood set along the border stones.

Katrin filmed in the dying light as the structure reached the height of the children, who then stuffed it full of kindling. A match was struck and in a matter of minutes they had a conflagration.

Campers sat on benches, folding chairs, stumps, and logs. The temperature dropped and someone came around offering hot cider and donut holes. The men continued to drink O'Doul's, so Katrin snuck one for herself from a nearby cooler. They weren't giving her much to work with, and after having successfully captured a few gigs of B-roll, she slipped the strap over her shoulder to keep her camera on her hip.

There wasn't a script to work with, but she couldn't shake the feeling she was screwing around. And she did not screw around. That wasn't her, not when there was a job to be done.

Was it her nerves? Was she actually concerned about a group she'd convinced herself was perfectly harmless? Or was she still just plain burnt out, even under the best circumstances she'd created for herself in months? Cory was a willing grunt and gopher, but that meant passing off work she needed for getting back in the groove. It wasn't just that, though. Her focus was off. She missed the opportunity to shoot the amphitheater in its golden hour drowse, and that wasn't because she handed off the task.

Her eyes wandered to the curved stick that loomed over the congregation. It charted a volley toward the massive bonfire, its underside turned orange by the firelight. They had to do something with it tonight, but so far no one paid it any attention. There was nothing, not one remotely peculiar thing, going on.

Guilt and urgency building inside her, she went to Sandy, who spoke with some of the women from the parking lot, to say she was going to wander the compound for additional footage.

"But it's so dark, and you've already filmed so much," Sandy said. She frowned, which in the firelight made her look dreadfully old.

Katrin clapped her mouth shut right as she was about to respond, noticing the other women twisting their necks in all directions. It was as if they heard a wolf howl deep in the woods, scouting the horizons for threats. Sandy held up her hand, which effectively redrew their attention.

Katrin watched Sandy, anticipating more strangeness to come, until she realized she was being offered the chance to speak. So she told Sandy, "You'd be surprised what you can capture in the dark, as long as you have a keen eye."

"There's a seat ready for you when you're back." Sandy passed off a wince as a smile, and gestured toward an Adirondack chair that was far larger than any others, and clearly situated in a place of honor, along with its twin. She nearly declined the offer, thinking the chairs were for Sandy and Ralston. Then Cory flashed into her head, and her stomach knotted again.

She wandered the compound, drawn like a moth to spotlights over doors and string lights drawn along trailheads, anywhere with light to work with. Buildings she shot low, making them loom in the frame, increasing the mystery of what went on inside them. Light strands she shot disappearing into the distance, leading into dark unknowns. If only the HSF gave her one bizarre thing to work with this weekend, she could pay off the hokey cinematography. On the other hand, she knew to be careful what you wished for.

After shooting every building in the compound, and the bonfire from a distance, what she really wanted was the sun. Night shooting with her prosumer camera wouldn't get her groove back. She was bored. Give her some daylight to play with. If there was one strong, borderline snobbish, conviction she had, it was that the sun should play a part in filmmaking. Not that she didn't appreciate the freedom and the painstakingly achieved contrasts of a studio set, or the joy of screwing around with whatever artificial light was at hand, but to the starting filmmaker, the sun was your god. The camera was a machine that worshipped it. It opened itself up, and there was only one thing worth putting inside. Light. There were no movies without it.

More gigs recorded, she went back to the fire, waiting for the torchbearers to return.

When she got closer, she saw, standing behind her chair, Sandy, Wendy, and two of the parking lot women. Katrin hadn't talked to Wendy since the move-in, and she actually welcomed the chance for some light banter. It might help wind her down for the night.

Only, when she came upon them, Sandy was frowning, and one of the parking lot women spoke in hushed tones about organizing search parties for the 'light-bearers'.

They didn't notice her approach, and driven by a fear that something had happened to the torchbearers, and Cory along with them, she asked if something was wrong.

Perhaps the women were jumpy, or perhaps Katrin had been slinking around more softly than she thought, but when they glanced over their shoulders, their eyes bulged and Sandy squeaked in surprise.

"Have Ralston and the others made it back?" she asked. Her domineering spirit kicked in.

Let's not waste time. What can I do?

The women scrutinized Katrin. Her words spiraled like a marble in a funnel, and only when it finally reached the drain hole did Wendy throw up her head in understanding.

"Oh, goodness! I thought *you* were telling *us* something went wrong. No, they're not back, but they're hardly late. There's nothing to worry about. That's exactly what I'm trying to tell the girls."

"Are you sure? I could come look if there's a

problem," Katrin said, looking at the two strange women, trying to form a rapport. The torchbearers probably went in the same direction every time, but they wouldn't necessarily expect her to know that.

"Absolutely not. It's fine," Wendy insisted.

"Well, you know what I think about the mountain lions," said one of the parking lot women. Her words came out stagey, like a disapproving matriarch in a play.

Sandy sighed. "We've said it a thousand times, Dee. The men never go out alone, and you know that's what lions are looking for."

"So we're okay?" Katrin asked.

Dee scrunched her face in a banishment of uncomfortable thoughts, then mumbled, "Fine." She walked away, giving a hurt look to Katrin.

Sandy came to her side, put a hand on her shoulder. "Just nerves, that's all. Some folks forget how wild it can feel up here, and it reminds them of news stories. That kind of thing is very rare, and it never happens here."

Wendy pulled her under her arm, stealing her from Sandy's touch. Another surprise. Katrin didn't really mind. "Time for an honesty check. Dee actually brought it up right when you left. She was worried you might go too far and get lost, and I was, like, have you met this girl?"

Katrin smirked, though her mood didn't match it. Wendy was kinda like Nira, if Nira astral-projected into another person's body to have her back from afar.

"You weren't in any danger. Did you feel like you were in danger?"

She shook her head. The awkwardness was hard to ignore, and as its main source, she didn't really know how to dispel it.

With a little squeeze, Wendy released her. Katrin took her place in the Adirondack, and Wendy ended up sitting next to her, though not in the other Adirondack. She asked Katrin all the same things everyone else did, then moved on to some more entertaining gossip.

Katrin was given a cider. The sight of it made her bladder bulge, and she crossed her legs to hold it in. She couldn't make herself get up. Not until Cory got back and vanquished the mental image of him being mauled by a mountain lion.

7

A hoot, some whoops, then a round of applause rose from the campers. Out of the dark came a bobbing flame. The torchbearers were back.

Katrin sat forward and found Cory in the middle of the group. He smiled. One of the men spoke into his ear and another chucked his shoulder. The others dispersed, either to find a seat or visit their cabin.

Sandy guided Cory to his seat beside her. He didn't seem to find it strange, too caught up in the fanfare. Ralston came up behind Katrin, and put up his hands to tamp down the noise.

He looked first at Cory, then Katrin, and winked. "The lighting of the way is complete," he announced.

Polite approving claps, a couple whoops.

"The light follows the light. It will find its way here."

The clapping intensified. Cheers arose. Before they reached the same heights as when the torchbearers returned, a man called from the crowd. Katrin jumped at first, and stared into the mass of people looking for the disruption.

"Zenith! Zenith!" cried the man.

Ralston cupped his hands to his mouth. "Yes! What, ho!"

"Zenith, leader and friend. The light will find the way. But how will it know where to stop?"

"We will show it!" Ralston cried.

He held out his arm. The man holding the last lit torch stepped forth.

Chair fabric groaned and metal clattered as campers on the other end of the fire got up and cleared a path leading to the curved stick. Another man kneeled down a few feet away and lifted a box off the ground, then turned a handle. He nodded to the torchbearer, who held the torch at the bottom of the concave side of the stick that faced the fire. With a whoosh and a flash, a new flame erupted at the stick's base. The man moved the torch up the length of the stick, causing new little fires to burst into life. He ended at the tip, which practically pointed at Katrin and Cory, making a final, large flame leap up to the sky. After a moment, the whole stick was engulfed in flames.

"Zenith! Zenith!" again cried the man.

"What, ho!"

"The light knows it may rest here."

"The light follows the light."

The crowd erupted into lively cheers and applause.

Katrin leaned into Cory once everyone rearranged their seating pattern to adjust to the second new blaze. "How was your walk in the woods?"

"About what you'd expect. Every few hundred

yards we stopped to plant a torch. Then they did a recitation kinda like that, lit it, and moved on, until we got to a ledge at the far end of the trail. Only Ralston talked at that one, but it was private. I don't know what he said."

"Did they leave the torches burning?"

Cory shrank away from her and looked embarrassed. "Well, they put them all in clearings. And they're like oil-burning torches or something, so there aren't any sparks or embers."

You still get a look, thought Katrin, despite the fact he couldn't have stopped them even if he had the guts to try.

Before long, a board member gave a fifteen minute warning before the movie started in the pavilion. Another board member, the one who'd been talking up his son's film aspirations, leaned in between Katrin and Cory and said, "We'll see who's a real George Lucas fan tonight."

Once half of the campers had gone, they got up, too.

"Where you going?" Cory asked when she turned toward the cabins.

"Stretching my legs. I'll be there in a minute, torch boy."

She was sure he hesitated to go when she left him. But he had to go on his own at some point. She had something she wanted to do, and she wasn't going to tell him or risk doing it later when more people in her cabin would notice. For now she could claim she was on another little filming excursion.

The firelight spread across the compound and helped her find the pathway. Once she started down it she slowed to adjust to the dark. Then she pulled out her cell for its flashlight. Her battery was below fifty percent, and a single bar of service flickered on and off like a lick of flame.

Thoughts of mountain lions kept her ears on high alert, but with the reassurances of the nearby activity, the full passage of dusk, and Sandy's words, she pushed on, shivering against a cold breeze.

The whitish-blue flashlight showed where the trail opened onto the clearing. Its light unfurled patches of dusty dirt floor, its edges soaked in a dark void. When she looked up, she caught the torch's dying flicker over the amphitheater stage.

She ascended the bleachers one step at a time. When she reached the top, she checked the stability of the safety railing, then turned off the flashlight. Once her eyes adjusted, the lighter slate color of the sky showed the far mountains in relief, and stars came out of hiding to twinkle faintly at her.

A cigarette would really hit the spot. She fidgeted and licked her lips until they were chapped, craving one despite not having one on her. Who knew what the HSF would think.

She rocked against the railing and fed on the day's observations. The people were happy here. The ritualism, what she'd seen of it, seemed offhand. Was it just that hardwired into them that it seemed banal to her, or were they really just a social club with silly rules to spice things up and freak out the neighbors? She wondered if the rituals and beliefs came unbidden into the DiMarcos' heads. Was such a thing possible, or did Ralston's little call and response, for instance, entail trial after trial of sloppy revision before they arrived at the harmony she'd witnessed?

Common sense told her it was the latter. But was there any more transcendence hidden in the grind of inventing ritual than there was in any other arduous task? Were they really making something here that made people feel better?

Cory and she were here to look at the people at the center of this thing. That was the truth of the matter. Ralston and Sandy DiMarco had put in the work, and she was here to see its purported ministrations. Of course she wouldn't be welcomed by everyone. The women in the parking lot made sense when she realized the sanctity of their special place was a matter of survival. That's what made cults break down. Financial problems, health problems, family problems. There was no room for the inevitable ugliness of life in such places.

Katrin was that ugliness. An outsider intent on drawing attention to their suspension of disbelief. No one really wanted her to tell a story here. She didn't even know who the audience was for this thing. And because of that, it didn't compel her. She wanted to go home, but she knew what waited for her there.

That was enough heavy thinking for the night. She licked her lips, breathed deep the mountain air, and rolled her head on her shoulders, trying to detect a buzz. She acknowledged she couldn't, and said softly, "Screw it."

This would be tricky. And she had to go fast, because she had to go bad.

Here's to you, Tommy boy.

She took off her shoes, unbuckled her belt, removed her pants, and squatted on the top bleacher bench, facing the valley. Her arms held the railing like she was hanging from monkey bars. Hips pressed forward, she peed over the edge.

When she was done, there was one thing that startled her. As she hiked up her pants, out of the corner of her eye, she caught a glint of light in the darkness. It made her fall onto the bench and freeze her backside, thinking it was a flashlight, that someone had seen her. She looked toward the path, and saw nothing. She looked to the stage, where the torch was faded to a little blue orb. That was when she realized her disorientation. The light was brighter than that, and it came from the opposite direction. She looked out at the valley and saw a vignette of light over the horizon, like the last vestige of day. But that didn't make sense. She must have been looking at the torch's afterimage.

8

"You not sleep?"

It was eight a.m. and sunny, the amphitheater clearing showing off new patterns of shadow. Picturesque, and a meaningful location to the HSF. That made it good for video diaries.

Cory aimed a thousand yard stare straight at the stage. The hollows of his eyes were purple and puffy, and his cheeks drooped. "Nuh-uh. You?"

"A little. Mattress sucked and my back aches. It was quiet as a grave, though. Are you good otherwise?"

Cory's eyes flitted to hers. "Yeah. Good."

Katrin stretched her back and groaned. "You gonna fix that cowlick before the interview? It'll work for a diary, but you need to be put together when we meet Sandy and Ralston."

"Yesss."

"And you going to change?"

He pinched the breast of his billowing plaid shirt. "What's wrong with this?"

She shook her head. "You ever seen that movie last night?"

"Uh, yeah, of course."

"I haven't. Aaand, we're rolling. Action. So Cory, tell me, what's your first impression of the Highest Seeking Faithful now that you've spent a night in their compound?"

They took turns prompting one another, making observations about the group's cheeriness and teamwork, their impressions of Sandy and Ralston, their first glimpse of ritualism in the torch lighting and bonfire.

The morning light provided a dose of invigoration. Katrin got up with the women who were on breakfast detail, and she spent the morning reviewing the DiMarco interview before washing up and finding Cory out by the fire pit.

Diaries complete, they went back to their cabins, then met back up for breakfast in the pavilion. There, Cory, who hadn't changed his clothes, said Ralston offered his office in the main lodge for the interview.

"Perfect," she said, whether it was or not.

At this point, she wasn't surprised to find both DiMarcos ready and waiting when they showed up in Ralston's office at ten a.m. Their eagerness was clear, shoving aside paperwork, shooing away an assisting board member, and diving into discussion of set dressing. One more push to get some work done. Katrin needed it.

The office was as large as a classroom, fully finished, off-white, and southwestern styled. A sprawling oak desk sat under large latticed windows, a bookcase ran the length of one wall. Along the other, a sideboard, secretary desk, and huge Navajo tapestries. In the center was a sitting area with a couch, a pair of upholstered chairs, a pair of ottomans, and a coffee table. Red-and-white patterned wool rugs segmented the room and set a fiery foundation for the neutrals all around.

It was perfect. Plenty of space to work, all the natural light you could ask for, lots of soft stuff to break echoes, and furnishings fit to color the DiMarcos' personalities.

"Let's do it by the bookcase," Ralston said. He started for it, then stopped short and looked at them questioningly, like it wasn't his place to say. Katrin said she couldn't have picked a better spot, and Cory and Ralston situated the chairs by it. "I'd like to have our friend Andrew in the shot," he continued, which made Cory do a double-take. "This photo was taken the first time we came camping up here. I don't know if you know, but he passed on up here on a trip a long time ago. There wouldn't be a Highest Seeking Faithful without him."

Ralston pointed out more of his knickknacks. "This is his compass, and this is the mug he always brought camping. He was such a character. It was chipped back then, but he wouldn't throw it away. Said it was lucky. Now this here is interesting. It's a remnant of the first bonfire we had as the Highest Seeking Faithful." From its display easel, he picked up an attractive charred section of a branch that was preserved with a thick layer of resin.

It was all the easter eggs they could ask for. She scanned his books, which were jammed tight on every shelf, most of them academic looking, their print quality and titles all to some degree dubious to her. The place where they set the chairs was filled with vintage sci-fi paperbacks and old hardcovers without dust jackets, which was for the best, since it leant a sort of venerable-yet-nutty professor vibe. And it looked better on camera.

They moved a floor lamp to provide light from the room's interior, and Cory set up a reflector that gave needed illumination to the background. A couple folding chairs were retrieved for them. Once she was satisfied with the setup, she gave him a look. Gravely, he told the DiMarcos they were ready to start.

After making him suffer a moment, shaking a water bottle as she slowly gave their work a once-over, she concurred. It was a vital moment for him. The interview was off-camera, which was a blessing, but Cory was taking the lead. It was all part of his education, as far as she was concerned. They spent a full Saturday doing mock interviews to prepare, but now that they were here, his nerves gave her cause for concern.

The DiMarcos finished preening by the window, then sat down and examined their clothes for wrinkles. Ralston was in a solid blue button-down and Sandy in white with a brown vest. She fluffed her hair. He wiped his glasses with a handkerchief, then stowed them in his breast pocket after worrying about the glare. They leaned into one another with such habitual intimacy that Katrin thought they might hold hands.

Cory took a seat. She ran the camera, turned on the microphone, and held up the clapperboard.

"DiMarco interview, day two. Roll one, scene one, take one," she monotoned.

The DiMarcos nestled into their seats and smiled wider.

Cory cleared his throat. "Could you please state your names and titles, please?"

The DiMarcos answered. Cory thanked them. Katrin clenched her teeth.

Just get a move on.

He asked what was the Highest Seeking Faithful, and the pair answered one after the other, Ralston with the group's stated mission, Sandy expanding on its humanitarian ambitions.

Cory murmured an acknowledgement. Katrin glanced sidelong at him, and saw the legal pad with the printed interview shaking in his hands. She had a copy in her own lap. *Take it easy*, she silently imparted. There was little to do besides keeping the DiMarcos gabbing. She would jump in if she had to, if they evaded questions. Her one dark hope was that Ralston, under the fawning spotlight, proved to be his own worst enemy once he got going, and spilled some particularly outrageous secrets. Her hope, Cory's assumption. It wasn't going to happen. She didn't think either DiMarco would delineate the HSF's activities any more deeply than they had for the public. Neither she nor Cory were trained interviewers. They weren't going to get any gotchas. Prompt them, let them ramble.

Cory mumbled through a couple more questions, including a follow-up. She settled back in her seat. He wasn't particularly charismatic, but his audio wasn't meant to be used, and the DiMarcos were cooperating.

She checked on him again when she noticed his breathing. She hadn't noticed when they started, but his nostrils were hissing loud enough for her to hear. His face was red and sweaty, and his chest rose and fell in big, uneven intervals. She reached for the water bottle at her feet, and passed it behind the tripod. He didn't notice, and moved onto the next question.

"The Highest Seeking Faithful is classified as a 501(c)3 organization, correct?"

"Yes, that's correct," Ralston answered.

Katrin furrowed her brow. Still holding the water, she looked at her lap.

Tell us how the Highest Seeking Faithful began.

He skipped a question. Actually, he made one up.

"Would you care to comment on the allegations of financial mismanagement that have been made in recent months against the Highest Seeking Faithful?"

Um.

Katrin didn't just stare daggers. She hauled out her longsword and held it to his jugular. "Cory," she said.

"Oh," said Ralston. He interlaced his fingers and gave a quizzical look. Not at all offended. "What are these allegations?"

Cory peeled up the bottom corner of his legal pad, as if reminding himself of the specifics of some particular footnote. Katrin recognized the douchebag move for what it was. "Misappropriation of funds set aside for educational scholarships, if my notes are correct."

One of Thomas's accusations. How did he even remember? It was one of dozens, literally hundreds, of crimes that idiot had rambled on about. Jesus Christ. Why wasn't her mouth working? Obscenities were fine, weren't they? She'd never known a stern look to cut it, but she froze, and that's all she had to throw at Cory as he turned up his nose at the DiMarcos.

"Oh, I don't think so," Ralston said with a philosophical air.

"You don't promise to pay tuition and other fees

for members' children to go to college?" Cory asked, more focused than Katrin had ever seen him.

"Oh, dear, no," said Sandy, far more perplexed than her husband, looking to him and Katrin both for an explanation. "We only wish we could help with college tuition, but the organization doesn't have that kind of money. We have our spiritual curriculum onsite. And I suppose we provide stipends to our administrative interns at the Fresno headquarters, if that's what you're referring to. But that's only a couple every year, and we've never heard any complaints. And believe me, we would if there were any. They've all come from very involved families."

"Nevertheless"—Cory turned to Ralston—"do you find it unusual to endorse a glorification of what you apparently call 'stupefaction', while at the same time claiming to support personal betterment, spiritual growth, and the pursuit of higher education?"

These were scripted. Katrin was still frozen, but her rage peaked, and before she put a stop to his nonsense, she cast a vicious, thorny shadow over the room, sure that all three of them felt it snatch away the light and the warmth.

Ralston sat back with his hands in his lap and set his gaze to the floor. Sandy, not at all shy, pressed on. She wrung her hands between her thighs. "We offer educational excursions sometimes, and our team building classes incorporate lessons based on where they occur, like nature or history subjects. And sometimes members like to help each other pay for special courses for their children. But, often, mostly, I mean, really all the time, that's handled outside the bounds—"

"Sandy." Ralston placed a hand on his wife's

armrest.

His interjection gave Katrin back her voice. The chaos was rampant enough to unfreeze her. "Mrs. DiMarco, please excuse this line of questioning. I think—"

"—just members helping members. I couldn't conceive of an instance in which funds would have been... uh, miscalculated or, what was your word for it? What have people been saying about..."

"So the funds are set up without any intent of actually using them for education," Cory asserted.

"*Cory.*" She stood up. She shut off the camera.

"Sandy." Ralston gently placed his hand on his wife's leg. "I think there is a misunderstanding that could use clearing up before we move on. I suggest we all stop what we're doing and get to the source of the issue before we start making things up and making ourselves upset."

"No, I don't think that's necessary," Katrin said. She wasn't about to put her hand on Cory's leg, but in her head she squeezed it until blood vessels popped. "If you'll excuse us a moment, I'd like to speak with my partner." She gave the DiMarcos a knowing look, willing them to know whose side she was on. "Cory," she intoned.

Cory's set expression faltered. His face de-aged fifteen years. Outnumbered, he looked small. A stubborn anger smoldered in his eyes, but his mouth trembled. He got up, avoiding looking at the DiMarcos.

They were halfway to the door when Ralston said, "Before you go, I'd like to speak to a point that's been raised."

"We won't be two minutes. I apologize," said Katrin. She was being generous. It would only take thirty seconds to cut Cory down to size.

"No, no, please. I insist. Before we move on to other topics. Is your camera running? The little red light isn't on."

Katrin stepped up and started recording at his encouragement.

He didn't wait for them to sit. "You mentioned stupefaction. And if there's one misunderstanding I can clear up now, it's regarding that. As a matter of fact, most members have a problem with it when they first join. And I still get teased about it." He nodded at Sandy. "Even by her! When we started out, I used 'idiocy', plain and simple, to describe this thing that we strive for, if you believe that. And I can tell you that it did not help us make friends. But I liked the attention it got, and the dissonance it created in people as they struggled to understand how to strive for something that by nature requires no striving. So I changed from idiocy to a word that grabbed people's attention without provoking as much ridicule.

"Of course, that was before we realized we're not striving for this thing. By nature, we can't. So we dropped the phrasing, too. 'Striving for stupefaction'. 'Working toward stupefaction'. By nature, you cannot strive for that which can't be striven for. Stupefaction can't be achieved.

"So it stands on its own. No explanation. Only the luckiest of us will ever experience it. We've certainly seen it. Everyone can. It's in the sun. And it's in the mountains here. I know I came up here looking for something, but it came looking for us, too. And knowing about it is quite painful for us. As painful as not knowing about it. We wish we didn't know, that we weren't just… *in the know*. We *want* stupefaction."

He cleared his throat, swallowed back the phlegm,

and scratched his nose.

Katrin wasn't sure how to respond.

Sandy read her expression, then leaned into her husband and said, "I don't think that quite answers the question, dear."

"Oh." He jolted and smiled, self-seriousness gone. His eyes searched the air while he recalled Cory's comments. "Stupefaction is entirely separate from our thoughts on education, which are positive. It has nothing to do with, oh, anti-intellectualism, I suppose, contrary to how it might sound. How about that?"

"Yes, I think that makes sense," Katrin said. "Sorry. One moment."

She forced Cory out the door.

9

Smile for the people in the lodge. Pretend everything's fine. Check that office. Busy? Occupied?

Oh, sorry, just looking for the kitchen.

How about the next office? Empty? Yes? Excellent. No one inside. Just shove the little dummy in and lock the door.

"You…" she searched her database with held breath, "dumb fuck." It was a miracle her bottled water didn't explode, she clenched it so hard.

Cory puffed out his chest. No longer outnumbered, he wheeled on her and said, "What?"

She wanted to shove him, but the old professionalism kept her in check. "Keep your voice down. You're done today. You do not attack them like that. You do not speak to them or anybody else. I am going back in there alone, and for the rest of the day, you will film group activities from afar. I will do the hard stuff."

"Why? This is what we're here for, Kat. These

people—"

"Do not call me Kat."

"What is your problem?"

"You going off script and nuking the interview. Nuking the project, while we're at it. We did not come up here to fuck around."

"This is the project. That's what I'm saying. We came here to ask them about all the shit they're accused of, just like the Instruments—"

"Oh sure. On the first morning here, without any proof, all guns blazing."

"You've told me millions of times about this Thomas guy, and the people who've disappeared. Ralston himself pointed out Andrew. And that reminded me. I swear I heard him mention Andrew last night at the last torch. Remember that guy? The first to go missing? Their cult is, like, built on his bones or some shit."

"Thomas's word counts for nothing."

"Says who?"

"Says me, when he turned out to be a total creep. When no one else could corroborate what he was saying. When our own research netted us nothing. When the only other remotely legitimate attempt to look into the HSF was with a local Fresno news crew, and they ended up with a feel-good story about a mobile food bank when they wanted to find virgins dog-chained in a basement."

"No one is going to find that."

"Yeah, I know. And I know you know. You came out swinging with financial impropriety instead of missing bodies. You won't find either one here." She had to tell him. It would shut him up, and this was dragging on longer than she wanted. She had to pull him back to reality. It was insane to think an organization like this would let in the wolves to rip out their guts from the inside. The morning's verdict was that he didn't get a say anymore. It was that simple. It was time.

"So you don't believe any of it," he said.

She took a deep breath, grateful this was coming at a time when she was incapable of remorse. "The DiMarcos have final cut. We are here to interview them, learn about the HSF, assemble a documentary feature, and present it to them for approval."

Now that she said it, she wondered how much could be heard through these walls. Ralston's office was in here so they had to be thick enough for confidential matters. She wondered if she was willing to clap her hand around Cory's mouth if he lost it.

"What..." he began. His voice was low, but it seethed with anger. His eyes went unfocused, searching beyond the walls. His face grew redder. "What, what do you mean, final cut?"

"If you wanted this project so bad, we had to be above board. I signed a contract with them. And, honestly, this shouldn't be a surprise. I only formalized what was obvious from the beginning. They'd have to be out of their minds to let us waltz in here, embarrass them, and waltz back out with the footage to show it."

And we'd have to be out of our minds thinking we were exposing the next Heaven's Gate.

Cory was speechless. That rarely happened with crew members on Katrin's sets. Everyone had an excuse or an argument. They always lashed out.

Her temper lowered. "Look, you can't come at people like this. And if you do, you need more than some half-assed alleged-this, accused-that, and 'some shit'."

She waited to see if he had a response, if she had to ramp her fury back up. She was about to lay down how things would work from now on when he went to the corner and faced the wall.

"Cory, what is it?"

"I know we're not going to find any bodies or whatever here. I *know* that. But you won't let me finish."

"What's there to finish?" She pulled out her phone and checked the time. It'd only been a few minutes, but they had to move. The DiMarcos weren't going to wait around, especially after that display of disrespect.

Still turned away, he said, "You think the Instruments wasn't just like this?"

"You know I wasn't actually there."

"I know that!" he shouted.

She flinched. Her eyes made for the door.

"They don't need to have bodies hiding around to be capable of the same shit the Instruments did to us. And I know you weren't there. But your parents were, and look how fucked up you are as a result. You wanted to come here, too. You were too curious not to. And if there's anything I can do short of killing someone to keep it from happening to anyone else, I'll do it." He turned around. "But now... we're making a *recruitment* video for them?" The color in his face had drained. He threw out his arms, which then flopped down to his sides.

She stepped closer and looked out the window. Seeing the outside helped her keep her cool. "These aren't the same people, Cory. I know what your family went through, and that it's still messing with your head, but you're not going to make up for it like this. I don't know if you expected some sort of cleansing or catharsis to happen, but I'm also not convinced you're going to take down another bad guy by coming here. I haven't been convinced of that for quite some time."

He shook his head. Tears streamed down his cheeks. He wiped them away, tried to put his one great vulnerability back inside, having squandered his righteousness at the wrong time and the wrong place. He went to the window and leaned against the sill. "This is exactly what Instruments was like. It felt just like this. Everyone was smiling. Everyone was happy and getting along…"

Until the ugliness showed up, the disbelief was suspended…

"…until they learned who that guy really was, and what he was able to make people do."

She thought of her own life, cast in the shadow of a con artist, the effects of his malice so deeply embedded in her parents that they shielded her from everything. Told her to trust no one, not even them.

What is it that matters to you?
The kinda thing my parents got suckered into.

It wasn't even her thing. It was her parents'. It was Cory's. It was stupid to think she was doing this for herself. Maybe she'd never find a way to make sense of her problems, but what wouldn't she give to understand why your life could be so damaged by a single person you'd never met. That shouldn't be allowed.

The more she thought about it, the more she realized all they'd done by coming here was to tear apart the scars that had already formed.

She went to him and handed over the water. He took it and drank without hesitation. Good kid.

"Take a few minutes, okay? I'm going back in there to smooth things over. But from here on out, I run the show. Let's salvage what we can today and start fresh tomorrow. I think we're lucky the DiMarcos acted as graciously as they did." She let the disappointment creep back into her tone. She had to focus on the job. So did he. She left him gazing out the window.

When she reached Ralston's office, Sandy burst out of the door.

"Change of plans!" Sandy announced, back to her bubbly self, marching straight for the doors. "The forecast is calling for rain this afternoon, so we're rescheduling our hike to start now."

Katrin hurried to catch up and began stammering a response, but Sandy kept going.

"We can pick this up this afternoon, I promise. We don't get a lot of leeway on these short weekends, so that's just how it goes. Come film it, though, please!"

Katrin blurted an okay and then, to herself, murmured that she'd get Cory.

She didn't want a change of plans. She wanted to know how things stood now. But she couldn't have been given a clearer answer. And now that Cory knew the full story, knew where things really stood, what other option was there?

She couldn't help fighting it, though. It wasn't hard to remember what waited for her back home. Nira's couch. Nira's disappointment. Weddings. The hustle. That was her future.

The project was dead. This was the last weekend they were going to be here.

10

"Pack our shit. We're going out with the group now."

Cory's head recoiled. "Did they cancel the interview?"

"Postponed, they say. But I don't know. Sandy says rain's coming and they need to get out. I'll try to find out what the full plan is. Head back to the cabin and get ready to run and gun. I'll meet you by the fire stick thing."

She left him with a dumb stare on his face and half a bottle of water in his hand. She had to catch up with Sandy immediately, whether she could salvage this thing or not. She just needed to know. Could she stop a train wreck or not?

Ralston and Sandy were out of sight, but campers swarmed the cabins, coming from their breakout sessions, chattering loudly, many in bright white HSF t-shirts. There was never a dull moment. All part of a cult's machinations. If its leaders weren't sequestered in their private spaces, they would be at the center of everything. Katrin marched to the women's cabin.

Inside was like a massive backstage scene change. Everyone swapping gym clothes or casual wear, depending on what they'd been doing, getting into breathable, insect-proof, and ultraviolet-resistant hiking clothes. Louder than ever, their spirits high from whatever they'd been doing. Some girls sang a song they'd carried in from their session. One woman called out instructions to the room. Bug spray, sunscreen, stretch your calves, go pee, take a drink.

Halfway down the room was a long ponytail tied at the nape of a neck that Katrin recognized. She pushed through the crowd, squeezed between a pair of women, and stepped over a young girl crouched on the floor tying her shoes before she got to Wendy.

"Katrin! Are you ready? Oh, you're not ready. You'll sweat to death in those jeans. Where's your pack?"

"Yes, I will. But wait, have you seen Sandy? I need to talk with her." She felt like she was shouting.

"She's right behind you."

Katrin could barely turn with all the bodies around her. She swore there were more women in here than last night, like all the other cabins had come to change in here. She untangled herself from a cluster of teenagers moving in the opposite direction and called Sandy's name. Finally, at least for a second, she was free from the whirlwind.

"Hey Katrin, what's up?" Sandy came to her, placed a hand on her shoulder, and together they formed a little bubble, shielded from disruption.

She barely took a breath before she spoke. "I want to apologize for what happened back there. I'm sure that came as a total surprise. It was completely unacceptable and I—"

"Heads up!" A girl tossed clothes over them onto a top bunk. Another woman slinked behind Katrin and bumped her into Sandy when she crouched down to retrieve something beneath a bunk. "So sorry, so sorry," she said, hauling a bag out over top of Katrin's feet.

"Oh my goodness," said Sandy, clearly delighted by the action. "You were saying?"

"I was saying that I want to apologize for how you were treated back there. It was completely unacceptable, and we didn't mean to make you worry about the direction of the project. I've spoken with Cory, and he was under the impression that you wanted to field some hard questions right away so you could address them directly."

Sandy was searching her face as she spoke, but when Katrin mentioned Cory she closed her eyes and shook her head, like she finally understood what Katrin was so worried about. She squeezed her shoulder. "We're not worried about that at all, dear. It's perfectly okay. That makes perfect sense. But you've spoken to him, yes? And he's okay? We could tell he was so upset."

Katrin paused. "Well, yes, I... He was upset with himself for causing you discomfort."

Sandy moved closer to Katrin to keep the aisle open as more women and girls filtered in or finished up and left. The woman behind Katrin kept her from making more space for herself.

Wendy pulled in beside them. "All good?" she asked.

The crouching woman finally got up and pushed past Katrin one last time. "Sorry, sorry, sorry."

Sandy let go of Katrin and pulled in Wendy for a half hug. And even though she stretched to reach over her friend's shoulder, she looked less tense than a second before, relieved by the passing of some huge source of stress. "Yes, all good. Katrin was worried about some movie business, but it's all okay. Her friend was very upset about it, and we were afraid he'd want to leave."

"Leave!"

"I know! So I assured her that everything is fine. They don't need to go until they're scheduled to go. And—oh, is that Ralston with him now?" Sandy leaned to look out the window.

Katrin shifted to follow Sandy's gaze, which was when she noticed a weight on her foot.

She didn't think anything of it at first. It felt like the ghost of a touch from when the crouching woman struggled with her bag. It's not like the woman bumped her hard, but the pressure of the bump was still there. Katrin had been busy focusing on Sandy, tuning out the cabin noise.

The weight was permanent now. It wasn't the memory of a touch. A shackle was clasped around her ankle.

"Uh," she said.

"Anyhoo, I gotta scoot and brief the trail leaders. Wendy, can you fill Katrin in on the rest of the weekend?"

Katrin stared at her. Someone else came by. A beaming smile flashed at Sandy. Katrin's duffel was in another woman's arms. A hot ball gathered in her chest and her legs went wobbly. The world turned white, and Sandy and Wendy were at its center.

Wendy jumped like she'd remembered something important, then whispered to Sandy.

Katrin gripped the bed frame and lifted her foot to

see if the shackle was really there. Its chain clinked against the floor and disappeared under the bed. It was hard to believe it was real. It was hard to know it was a shackle without knowing what she was shackled to.

"What... I..." Katrin looked up.

Sandy was gone, which left only Wendy, frozen mid-speech, her mouth shaped like an O, before she started droning on about upcoming meal times.

The flurry died down. The same few women who'd left the cabin yesterday finished tightening their laces, then they shouldered backpacks and left the bunkhouse without one backward glance, chitchatting all the way. Now that she looked, all the women had taken at least some of their bags, presumably with all their necessary belongings. Only Wendy remained.

"What the fuck?" Katrin blurted.

The chain slithered and hissed, and then, as she staggered away from the bunk, tightened with jealous ardor.

Wendy regarded her with a shocked expression that might've shriveled into guilt. Instead, she broke out a new smile bordering on lunatic. "Like I was saying, Griffin will be handling meals and everything before you leave. Everything goes through Griffin."

"Wendy." Katrin walked until the chain stiffened and tripped her. Wendy was out of reach anyway, having backed away as she'd talked. "*Wendy.*"

But Wendy was gone. The door was closed. Bolts slotted into place. A padlock dangled against the wood.

In less than a minute, and with nothing else about the day having perceptibly changed, Katrin was trapped. Outside was broad daylight. Hundreds of people were around. It didn't feel dangerous. She wasn't alone, right? She wasn't alone. That's what was dangerous. There were people here. Just normal people.

All she could think was that her back still ached from sleeping on a shitty mattress ten feet away.

Daylight faded. The storm Sandy said was coming never came. Only the slow closing eyelid of dusk.

Someone has to blow the lid off these guys.

Tell me about it.

Or you know what, maybe not. If people are stupid enough to stay and let themselves get castrated and waste all their money, fuck it. Let them get screwed.

Asshole.

Maybe someday enough of them will figure it out and crucify the DiMarcos on their own limp-dick stick.

Thomas again.

It was the call on which he'd articulated the group's perversions. They were feminist sheep, didn't you know. Sandy had Ralston wrapped around her little finger. They got God upside down, put the pussy on a pedestal. Sexual rites? They wish. They wouldn't know what to do with them. Coulda whooped Ralston's ass and taken Sandy for myself. Guy's chickenshit. She's worse but she's fucking hot for being old. Drinking the donor blood, right?

She could barely keep up.

I don't know why I'm telling you this. It's tailor-made for chicks. It was practically built on a male sacrifice. That Andrew guy? Sacrifice. Sacrifice after sacrifice after sacrifice, and they only get bigger after each one. What do you have against them, anyway? Or do you put being a pretend-journo before being a girl?

It was their last call.

It was the call that convinced her the HSF wasn't

worth investigating. When she hung up, she laid her head on Nira's kitchen table and watched her pen roll off its edge.

She was in the middle of cobbling together a demo reel, wondering if it was too late to get in on the wedding season, when Cory called.

11

Cory.

She screamed his name until she was hoarse.

They came and locked the windows from the outside. Glazed, security mesh installed. She missed that trick. They never took her phone, so they knew she didn't have service, which was true. Left her keys, too, which meant her car was as good as dead, if there was any chance of breaking out.

Sounds of chopping and hacking filtered through the walls. A match flame grew into a massive blurry orb of fire through the windows, and what should've been night turned into day. Another bonfire. A yellow sickle rose above it, the DiMarcos' limp-dick stick. Shouting now. Shadows marched across the light, obscuring the bottom fringe of fire, the entirety of the cult—not campers anymore, a cult—walking its perimeter. A mean little voice in her head said that Cory was out there with them. Maybe even Thomas, a double agent all along.

Griffin came to deliver dinner. The kid with the

camera.

He was tragically awkward, like a high school sophomore, probably actually a high school sophomore, but aging in reverse.

"Man, do you get headaches up here at all?" he complained. He sat down a few bunks over, claiming a bout of nausea. He dabbed his nose to check for blood. Getting up, he shook his head and brought her a plate stacked with steak and steamed vegetables. Hearty, sure, but a downgrade from last night's high summer feast.

He had to be a calculated choice. It was just hard enough not to have a go at him. Another woman, definitely, she'd have a go, now that her mind was right. An older man, she'd have gone full Amazon, clamped onto whatever limb came first, bitten off a perfect oval of flesh and left a neat hole, its slopes like striations in a steak torn by a dull knife, visible only before the hole pooled with candy red blood.

How's that for feminist, Thomas?

Griffin sat down across from her, and she discovered she was too tired to try anything. An afternoon of self loathing and shrieking took it out of her. His nonchalance was a warning, too, that she could hurt him, kill him even, plus any number of HSF members, and she'd still lose.

"Take it away, please," Katrin said.

"Can you try like four bites?" he asked. "They gotta see that you're eating. And hey, you'll get headaches like me if you don't."

She squinted at him, mustering the will to grab him by the throat.

"Please? They'll want to see that you ate

something."

"Throw it in the trash, fucker," she said, coaxing a growl from her destroyed vocal cords.

He looked at the trash bin near the back door. "Oh," he said, "yeah, that could work." So he did that.

The bonfire glowed through the night. Shadows shifted, giving the fiery orb a more pronounced flicker. Blood soaked her sock and shoe after she attempted to pull her foot through the shackle. She stopped once the very touch of its metal felt like a hot poker to her achilles.

Griffin returned, absurdly, to announce lights out a couple hours later. He removed a pair of sunglasses. His shoulders were slumped, and he carried Katrin's camera.

She tucked her bloody foot behind her other and looked out the window. "Lights out? You got blackout curtains to help with that?"

"Oh," he said. He looked troubled.

"What?"

"It's just… I wish you'd eaten something. I don't want anything to go wrong."

When she didn't reply he sighed and bit his lip, looking at the trash bin.

"What do you think of the mirrorless?" he asked suddenly, holding up her camera. He sat down next to her. The extra weight on the mattress made them lean into each other. Their shoulders touched, and he shifted and turned red.

"It does what I need it to," she said.

"The Sonys I've tried don't play nice with Macs. Weird file formats. Super compact, though."

"Keep it if you want," she muttered.

He sat upright, his mouth hanging in confusion,

before he said, "Oh, wow. That's really generous of you."

Her mouth went dry. He'd expected to keep it regardless.

"Do you know how to color-correct?" he asked. "I'm always blowing things out and, like, totally going nuts with the contrast."

A question like that indicated an undisciplined dilettante. Not that she needed more evidence. Cory wasn't too dissimilar, but she'd done what she could in their short time together, reinforced the importance of fundamentals. It wasn't worth it now.

She swallowed hard. "It's called log. You have to shoot in log."

12

The chain was attached to one of the bunk posts. The frame was metal, its bottom edge sharp. She didn't really know one metal from another, but she knew the frame was thicker than the chain link, and that one had to be weaker than the other. She only hoped it was the chain.

As the fire blazed and shadows danced, she ground the chain against the frame, doing it the brute force way, the cost of which were blisters across her palms that burst and stung with a pulsing hatred. As she went, she wished for her multitool, her kit bag, anything within reach that might have had something to use.

Her shoulders burned. Her spine ached and complained, but she didn't quit. Maybe she should've eaten dinner and filled up on added calories, added exertions. Just as pointless of a thing to wish for. She worked herself into a stupor. After an untold period of time, her body wracked with pain, she fell backwards into the other bunk as the link snapped and separated her from the frame.

Her ankle free, her body protesting every movement, she stalked to the back of the cabin. Onto the next obstacle, unarmed and alone. Busting windows was out of the question, and the door was too well secured.

Before she could turn away she was stopped by a smell. The meat and veggies, still wet and warm, wafted from the trash bin. It made her mouth water. She knelt down and breathed deep through her nose. Griffin thought he'd be in such trouble if she didn't eat. Good. She hoped they noticed, saw that he failed in his one duty.

He'd trashed the whole thing. The remnants sat on a small pile of other rubbish. Before, the meat looked like several slices piled together on the plate. But thrown away, it retained its shape. Just one big hunk.

She reached in, the meat's remaining moisture climbing her knuckles, and lifted it out with her rubbed-raw hands. Same as with her metals, she didn't know her meat cuts. Couldn't pair shapes to names. Tenderloin, sirloin, flank, shank. She only knew what packaged meat looked like, flat red kidney beans sitting prettily on styrofoam beds under fluorescent-reflecting plastic wrap. This was nothing like those.

Doctors, dentists, consultants, lawyers... These people could afford a good cut of meat. They barbecued up a feast last night.

What she held was as large as a heart, greasy and yellow with fat, its outer edges hardly browned, the inner musculature looking more like salmon than livestock. The firelight gave it a slick burgundy sheen. Blood streamed down her wrist. Fat squished through her fingers like sea foam. A bone ran through the gnarled, shapeless lump of flesh, its edges frayed and charred. Newly sawed.

Katrin's mouth dropped open. Her brain shut off her taste buds, her olfactory senses, refusing to acknowledge what they deduced. A hideous laugh sounded in the depth of her eardrums, a laugh filled with macabre glee. Fat sloughed off between her fingers and the scent, already trapped inside her, unveiled its name.

The scent and the firelight and the cabin brimmed with mad delight as Katrin realized she was officially on her own.

Upon picking the first hollow spot between studs in the wall, she got down and pounded her heel against the fiberboard. On her final kick, the outside board's jagged edge sliced her calf like a filet.

She only just managed to stick her phone out of the hole, hoping it would get a signal, when they rushed into the cabin and carried her away against the blazing light of the fire.

13

Under the morning light, they carried her from a sealed room in the main lodge to a wooden wagon, something like an old horse-drawn police wagon or Victorian-era bathing machine. A conestoga might've been more on brand, given all the other western trappings, but then she would've ripped her way through the canvas and run away all over again. In here, she only had four walls and a roof. Thin slats were cut out near the tops of the walls. The wagon was new, too, its smell as bracing as a pine air freshener. To think Home Depot was close enough that the lumber still blushed.

Sometime around noon, by Katrin's reckoning, they came to re-bandage her leg. She looked longingly out the door, wishing she were on the opposite side of the farthest peak she could see.

A man brought stools and rested her leg on his as he wrapped gauze around her calf. In the cramped space the humidity rose, and she thought her exposed wound helped it happen faster. The air was tinged with a close, corporal wetness that made her feel indecent in the man's presence. When some blood dripped onto the wagon floor, he frowned.

"What's the matter? Worried it'll spoil the taste?" she asked. "Is this the smokehouse? Is that how you prefer to do it?"

He made brief eye contact through his flip-up prescription sunglasses and smiled, wry and embarrassed. Doctor Anthony Kozlowski. He was one of the HSF's most prominent figures, a senior board member. He had his own practice in Fresno. A place to be on Monday. Katrin had studied his face on his website, failing to find the crazy in it, failing to trust her misgivings, as she had done for everyone else, all the way up until the end. She couldn't help but blame Thomas for out-crazying her darkest suspicions, taking out his anger at the DiMarcos with outlandish tales colored by extreme bigotry, misleading her into thinking he was the worse of the two. But even he hadn't brought up this kind of savagery.

"That should do you," Kozlowski said. He pinned the bandage tight and patted her shin before making a swift exit.

Bullshit it'll do me. I need stitches, you fucking butcher.

She took a deep, shuddering breath and hugged her knees to her chest. Smokehouse? Sweet Jesus, what a joke. "That wasn't me," she whispered. Her words echoed back at her. The wagon's confines stuffed them back in her mouth like a gag, as if any peep that might come out of her was a cry for help, as if a cry for help would do any good out here.

The sun peeked through the slat over Katrin's shoulder, a bright cutlass shining on the wavy wood grain.

She tried bending her leg, fighting through the drowsiness of an overworked immune system. Besides a topical antibiotic that burned like hell, Kozlowski hadn't given her any meds. They obviously weren't keeping her around much longer, but if they were going to eat her, wouldn't they want to ensure the meat wasn't tainted?

Katrin listened for hours and heard no more activity. It had to be afternoon by the time footsteps announced someone's approach.

The door swung open to Kozłowski. The wagon floor came up to his chest, perfect height for a kick to the chin if only she was up in time.

He climbed the step ladder to get inside and turned around to grab the stools.

When she winced at his touch, he peered at her until she nodded for him to proceed.

She bent forward for a look out the door. Pointing straight at her was the fire stick. The wagon was situated directly over the fire pit. As she digested that fact, she noticed the shadows had changed. Either that or the mountains had turned, checking themselves in a cosmic mirror, using the sun as their spotlight. A sharp scent of smoky late afternoon wafted in. She hadn't realized how stuffy the wagon was.

Ribbons of soothing ice wrapped her legs as the gauze came unwrapped. Kozlowski made a hum of consternation and turned away to stuff the wad of used bandages in a plastic shopping bag.

She risked a look down. Her entire calf was purplish red and swollen, the wound shouting from her skin with white lips and a mouthful of mashed cherries. She clenched her hands and looked away.

Her sarcasm was all used up, her shame immense, to let herself get conned, to put up so little of a fight. To think it all stemmed from a rum-drunk joke about jungle tribes and meta documentaries, a joke that lived on in her captors' incongruities. The whole point was that the boring ones were the monstrous ones. These people with their strip mall haircuts, big-ass SUVs, athleisure couture, prescription eyewear. These weren't her kind of people, but weren't they really? Weren't they the kind of people she was supposed to feel safe around? Or at least share a society with?

There was nothing for her to say anymore, sarcastic or otherwise. Questions were useless. Begging was pointless. That was why, once Kozlowski had finished re-trapping her wound under a gauzy new chrysalis, and with his head turned to snap shut his kit bag, Katrin leapt up onto her good leg, pulled back her other foot, and swung it into the doctor's lower jaw.

With a loud crack, Kozlowski's head whipped back. Katrin had seen such a thing countless times in movies and on live sets, but he hadn't thrown his weight into an actorly feint. His head absorbed her momentum. It was a real kick, and it connected. She lost her balance and tipped on her side. A second later, so did Kozlowski.

Katrin's wound screamed. The numbing tendrils of a panic attack wriggled from her fingertips to her core and a hot coal sat on her chest. In that moment, her horror at what she'd just done was the only thing that existed.

And yet. Kozlowski's head moved. His fingers curled.

Katrin exhaled a long held breath. Sliding her bad leg around the doctor's body, she half crab-walked, half scooted past him until her legs dangled from the wagon. She leaned forward and checked to her left and right.

Not ten paces off, standing just out of sight from inside the wagon, was Ralston. He wore his Stetson. His drooping lips, combined with his paunch and ramrod-straight posture, made him look like a confused, overgrown infant.

Katrin slid forward and dropped to the ground, staggering sideways to favor her better leg. The sun bundled her in its warmth against the thin mountain air, and she took her first non-wood-scented breath in hours. Her aches intensified. Her wooziness worsened. She staggered out of the fire pit, coating her shoes in ash.

Without the option of her car, she made for the amphitheater path, following a vision of sliding gently into the valley and towards salvation.

Neither Ralston nor any of the others moved to stop her. They hardly had to try. Instead they scrambled to put on sunglasses.

A headache pierced her skull. Her gorge rose, and each of her organs was outlined by a singular, unique pain. Her back ached and hips hurt, her stomach was empty, her bladder was full. It was the price paid for being cooped up, injured, and without food, water, or hope.

She slowed and turned around at the sound of Ralston calling her name. She was hardly able to make him out. Everything was bright, like the light had moved to face her head on, the sun shifting noticeably, impossibly, since she started walking. The world glittered.

It was the dehydration. It spoiled more than one shoot she'd been on. Joshua Tree. Death Valley. LA itself. After enough amateur shoots with guys like Cory who subsisted on coffee by morning, Mountain Dew by day, and beer by night, she became the de facto water nazi on every set she worked. The sun was a god, but it was a killer, too.

Ralston moved to the wagon, his outline like a living lava lamp, a white-on-white ink blot.

She turned toward the path, pushed forward by a spare drop of adrenaline. It kept her moving straight, giving her something to focus on besides her howling leg and the brightness that cored her eye sockets like an ice cream scoop.

She reached the edge of the compound and went all the way down the narrow path unmolested. Looking down into the amphitheater, she fought a reluctance to proceed. The last stop on the tour. Their most sacred spot. But she liked it there. And the valley was just beyond. She stumbled down the hill and collapsed on the first row of bleachers, breathing hard, letting her leg scream it out and her nausea settle down.

Overhead, fluffy white clouds passed across a blue pasture, but as with the mountains, the clouds were lit funny, as if from the side, like the sun were lower than them.

Her eyelids fluttered, and she leaned over until she laid down on the bench. Just a little farther, and she could hide in the wilderness, make a clean break for it. She was more confident than she'd been all weekend. Then she closed her eyes.

This hadn't started with a joke at all. There was no more meaningful cause for her being here than her own desire. She didn't even want to blame the HSF. That was too easy. A cult had been to blame for everything in her life. She refused to believe this came about because of something she inherited from her parents, or because she felt forced to fix something for some helpless wannabes around her, even if she was a wannabe herself. This was her fault. Her responsibility.

A rattling sound made her stir. She looked up, and sitting next to her was Sandy DiMarco, holding out a water bottle and a pill bottle. Her hair was in a ponytail and her legs were crossed. Her top foot fidgeted and her lips pressed together as she picked at the plastic wrap around the pill bottle. She wore sunglasses fit for a nuclear test.

14

"Here," said Sandy, "it's ibuprofen." She said it like she wished she had better. She peeled the plastic off the bottle cap and cracked open the water.

Katrin didn't count out pills, just threw back the bottle and washed it down with a mouthful of water. After a moment, Sandy handed her a pair of sunglasses. She stood and held out her hand. Katrin took it, and together they walked back up the path, Katrin's arm draped over Sandy's shoulders. The sunglasses suppressed the light to a tolerable degree, but the pain remained and Katrin barely looked up.

"I'm sorry," Sandy said when they reached the halfway point. "This is the first time we've tried the whole locking-you-up thing. But the others have always been so eager to leave, and they get away before we can see them off."

"You're insane," Katrin said, wanting to see how reality reacted.

"Tell me about it." Sandy sighed. "We should've

checked with you first. And, um, Cory, is it? We were afraid of him going earlier than you and luring it away. We know you want to go, and I swear we're not going to stop you. It's just… timing."

There was talking ahead. They were close to the compound. She looked down and watched as Sandy's shadow and hers spun like clock hands. Sweat poured down the back of her shirt.

Sandy continued. "So many come and go without giving us a moment's notice. All we ask is to witness it. We know we can't have it. We just want to see. They didn't let us collect the finder's fee, you know what I mean? It's made us feel a little used."

The path widened back into the compound. Sandy led her right back to where she started.

Katrin risked a look up into the bright scene. Dr. Kozłowski sat up in the wagon, wearing sunglasses. He smiled. Blood ringed his mouth, and she wondered how many teeth she'd knocked out. He was bundled away before she had the chance to apologize, an urge she couldn't help and was glad she wasn't forced to suppress.

Sandy and Wendy lifted her into the wagon. Ralston supervised, saying they needed to hurry.

She crawled to the back on all fours. It was bright as day inside. The back wall danced with hazy shadows of her from multiple sources of light, or was it an all-encompassing one? She sat down, and found the answer out the door. A veritable spotlight shone through it. It was as loud as it was bright, and she barely heard Sandy, a thimble of gray against a backdrop of fire.

"Really soon!" Sandy shouted, like she knew the light was loud, too.

The door slammed shut. Katrin's eyes adjusted from white to red to the blond of the wood.

There was more shouting.

"We won't stop you… when the doors open, just come out…"

Katrin screamed, not a name, not a cry for help, but the only sound left in her, the one that was curled around the bundled emotions that drove her flight from the compound. It came out coated in rage and righteousness and desire.

"…just come out… and you can go…"

The roar of the light faded. Footsteps padded nearby. It was time to light the fire. Breathe it all in, she told herself. Let it suffocate you. Let the flames take the corpse.

Then there were slapping sounds against the side of the wagon. Hands. Lots of hands. The wagon rolled.

She tensed against the walls, her various pains spiking. Men barked orders. Another moment of ant-like collaboration.

The walls gave her fingers no purchase, so she bounced around the wagon before turtling on her back. She spun onto her stomach, hoping for more grip, when the wagon pitched forward and she slid into the door. She scrambled to her knees only to fall over with another push from the men outside. The wheels crunched against dry brush, and on all sides she heard the trampling of dead grass.

There was no question about it. They were guiding her down the amphitheater path.

After a slow climb up the rise along the path, she listened as the men attached a rope for easing her down the last steep section.

A song came from below, only to be interrupted by shouting. From the sounds of crushing leaves and twigs, the wagon crew fled in all directions.

A roar descended onto the wagon. Blades of white light entered all four slats and shone on the inner walls. The slats' edges turned black and smoldered. Just as quickly as the roaring light arrived, it retreated, replaced with a deep-voiced chant from all sides, and a higher, harsher song from below. Following more shouting, the final descent into the amphitheater began. Katrin endured it sitting backward, facing upwards with her back against the door.

The song was shrill and guttural at once. Spat-out plosives, sputtering fricatives, husky glottals emanating from a female-heavy choir. After a final "Heave-ho!" from the men, the wagon was pushed up an incline. She heard boards creak underneath and understood the wagon was onstage. The men joined in the song, adding a gravelly bass. A full choir, four hundred strong.

Katrin lay in place, her wrecked body worn out. She looked from one scorched slat to another, her mind wandering.

All those crazy stories. All those things Thomas said and Cory suspected. All the grief her parents went through and passed on to her. These people really were like the Instruments of the Scion. They were like everyone else. They had nothing special to offer. They knew there was something big out there, but they didn't own it. They couldn't give it to you. Any idiot could say there was something bigger than us out there.

Idiocy.

Stupefaction.

She came here on her own. And she knew what waited outside the wagon.

"…just come out… and you can go…"

What makes them so unique, Cory? Why not report on the Instruments?

Instruments is dead, isn't it? And it's been done. The thing about the HSF is that cults normally run on total delusion, right? Like, complete faith in their leaders. These people, though? They're weirdly sheepish about it, like they don't believe their own hype. They mention this stupefaction thing, but they barely seem to understand their own explanation.

Think maybe you're dealing with a shitty recruiter?

I don't think so. I think it's worth a shot. I want to feel like I've done something. Anything short of shooting that Scion asshole in the head.

I don't know. This doesn't get you any closer to making a superhero movie.

It's personal to me, you know? It's for my parents, and for Jacosta, too.

Yeah, I know, kid. It's for me, too.

She'd let him make the project his. She was just along for the ride.

The door opened.

A blanket of heat wrapped around her. She shielded her eyes and sat up. The spotlight was on her again.

The song became a cheer, something like she'd heard at an illicit playoff football game she attended senior year. The winning and losing sides of a semifinal Hail Mary pass rolled into one garbled roar.

"…just come out… and you can go…"

She scooted forward and slipped onto the stage.

The light rose higher, like it was on wires, higher than any rig she'd ever seen. Sweat beaded on her forehead and arms. The light reeled itself in, dampened like a polarized lens had been applied, and returned some color to the world.

The bleachers were full. Past the crowd, through the trees, the once-blue sky had gone black as night. Whatever light the earth was allotted had collected itself at this one point and left the rest in darkness.

Patterns of light and dark fell on the mountains as had never occurred before. Two members rushed the stage carrying buckets of slop. Katrin recognized the wet, charred remains, the melted plaid fabric glommed onto hunks of meat, and wondered what he'd done, how much he'd fought to deserve such a fate. They left the buckets in the wagon, the final motion in their desperate last-minute ritual of ingestion, and ran away in clouds of steam rising from their water-drenched clothes.

A corona of light was overhead. Another roar and the light turned white, erasing all color. It was a sliver, a cutlass, as thin as it was blinding. It flattened into a circle.

A new wall of heat fell upon her. It singed the hair on her arms. The light moved over the wagon and dropped. It scorched a hole in the wagon roof and entered its confines. Light telescoped out the open door and in less than a millisecond the wagon burst into flames.

She chirped, a short insane laugh, to see her prison destroyed, to see a core of white plasmic heat follow in her footsteps. To see that what chased her was so clearly out of anyone's control. That it couldn't give one shit about the cult assembled before it.

A lick of heat touched her hands. It entered her,

scorched her without her body registering the injury, a blade offering its handle to her, putting the killing power in her hand. To sheath it, or to melt into it. To wield it, or to join it. She was on the right end of it, but the sun was going to do what it meant to do regardless of which way she chose. If she ran now it would follow. If it fled she would never stop chasing it.

There was no longer a project. No more minuscule manipulations of cosmeticians and film students and cultists and online trolls and ruined parents. No more finding community in her work by barging in others' way. It was Katrin and the sun, led to one another.

She removed her sunglasses. The sun brightened at the compliment, and she opened her eyes wide to drink it in.

It showed itself to her, inviting her in. And she did the same. The circle rose from the ruins of the wagon and leapfrogged her, placing itself like a plate at the edge of the burning stage.

It was impossible to distinguish the audience's song from the sun's roar.

She pictured them before her, beyond the light, surrounded by a raging fire that would destroy countless acres of mountain forest. Ralston up front, his arms wrapped around Sandy, both looking radiant. Wendy clutching her husband's hands. Kozlowski his wife's. Griffin in the front row, beaming, his parents on either side. All thinking they'd been given what they'd been denied for so long. The gratitude of the sun, the chance to earn their keep, to see what they'd never have, to give the HSF its only real meaning. If only they knew the sun didn't care, and that their reward wasn't only meaningless but nonexistent. It didn't want them. It didn't need them. It gave them that pain they felt all the time, every day, for being in the know. She would deliver it personally from now on, but she wouldn't need to look at them when she did. She'd never have to think of them or anyone else ever again.

Katrin stepped onto the plate. Her shoe soles melted, her clothes caught fire, her hair curled and turned to fire. Blood gushed from her calf and sizzled in a pool at her feet. Her flesh melted and collapsed into the thin layer of light. She was a struck match, dispersed to vapor and hardened to a diamond, and she and the sun became together.

It was work without having to quest for it. It was peace without the pain of fighting for it.

They were a small god in the grand scheme of things. They were the master of cameras. They were the one that edited what was meant to be. The light giver and life maker.

They were the blade that cut the distance between all that was. The scythe that separated day from night. They were the one that carved the cosmos.

These weren't her people. None were. None ever were, and none ever would be. And the sun wasn't a small god on this rock. It was the biggest one.

ACKNOWLEDGEMENTS

If not for the constructive criticism and encouragement of Mark Tullius, this little book wouldn't be what it is today. In fact, it wouldn't be here at all. And if it weren't for the constant faith shown by my wife Jammie, there's no telling how few words I'd have committed to the page in the first place, even if those words give her the heebie-jeebies. Thanks to you both.

ABOUT THE AUTHOR

P.W. Feutz is an author of horror in all its varieties. "The Sun Is A Circle Meant For Serving" is his first published book. He lives in Michigan with his wife and two rabbits, Sherl and Watson.

Printed in Great Britain
by Amazon